Chasing

THE LIFE JOURNEYS OF
HARRIET TUBMAN

Freedom

SUSAN B. ANTHONY

INSPIRED BY HISTORICAL FACTS

BY

NIKKI GRIMES

ILLUSTRATED BY

MICHELE WOOD

ORCHARD BOOKS • NEW YORK
AN IMPRINT OF SCHOLASTIC INC.

For my lifelong friend, Debra Jackson, a strong woman in her own right —N.G.

For my Lord Jesus Christ and my cousin Layla Gold —M.W.

We gratefully acknowledge Mary Huth and Ellen K. Wheeler from the National Susan B. Anthony Museum & House
as well as Kate Clifford Larson, PhD, for their astute, generous, and meticulous fact-checking of the text.

Photograph on page 50: *Susan B. Anthony,* Bain News Service/Library of Congress.
Photograph on page 51: *Harriet Tubman (between ca. 1860 and 1875),* H. B. Lindsley/Library of Congress.

Library of Congress Cataloging-in-Publication Data

Grimes, Nikki, author. Chasing freedom : the life journeys of Harriet Tubman and Susan B. Anthony, inspired by historical facts / Nikki Grimes ; [illustrations by] Michele Wood. — First edition. • pages   cm • Summary: In this imaginative biographical story, Harriet Tubman and Susan B. Anthony sit down over a cup of tea in 1904 to reminisce about their struggles and triumphs in the service of freedom and women's rights. Includes bibliographical references. • ISBN 978-0-439-79338-4 • 1. Tubman, Harriet, 1820?–1913—Juvenile fiction. 2. Anthony, Susan B. (Susan Brownell), 1820–1906—Juvenile fiction. 3. Women slaves—United States—Juvenile fiction. 4. African American women—Juvenile fiction. 5. Underground Railroad—Juvenile fiction. 6. Suffragists—United States—Juvenile fiction. 7. Feminists—United States—Juvenile fiction. 8. Women's rights—United States—Juvenile fiction. [1. Tubman, Harriet, 1820?–1913—Fiction. 2. Anthony, Susan B. (Susan Brownell), 1820–1906—Fiction. 3. Slavery—Fiction. 4. African Americans—Fiction. 5. Underground Railroad—Fiction. 6. Women's rights—Fiction. 7. Women—Suffrage—Fiction.] I. Wood, Michele, illustrator. II. Title. • PZ7.G88429Ch 2015   813.54—dc23   2014014835 • 10 9 8 7 6 5 4 3 2 1   15 16 17 18 19 • Printed in Malaysia   108 • First edition, January 2015 • The text type was set in Adobe Garamond Pro. • The display type was set in Dalliance Roman and Dalliance Script. • Art direction and book design by Marijka Kostiw

Michele Wood's paintings were created using acrylic and oil paints.
They were inspired by numerous symbols, geometric designs found in American
patchwork quilts, and African motif patterns.

Table of Contents

Harriet Tubman and Susan B. Anthony   8

Beginnings   10

The Call   12

Frederick Comes to Dinner   14

The Underground Railroad   16

Speech! Speech!   18

Rumors of Angels   20

The Right to Speak   22

Storyteller   24

Raising a Ruckus   26

Close Call   28

Frozen Footsteps   30

A Man Named John   32

All in the Family   34

Bounty   36

Unfettered   38

Drums of War   40

Confrontation   42

Call to Arms   44

World Afire   46

End of the Beginning   48

Biographies   50

Additional Notes   51

Bibliography   52

Author's Note   53

Harriet Tubman
and
Susan B. Anthony

It is 1904, a year in which the 28th Annual convention of the

New York State Suffrage Association met in Rochester, New York.

On this occasion, Susan B. Anthony will introduce the guest speaker,

the legendary Harriet Tubman.

That November afternoon, there was a rap at Susan's front door. Susan finished lacing up her shoes, then crossed the parlor in the staccato rhythm of one who's got places to go. Were it not for an abundance of white hair, you'd never know how many years she'd been on this earth, how many lives she'd lived. But there was one who could count them, one whose stories were river deep. Susan reached the door, swung it wide, and smiled.

"Harriet!"

"Afternoon, Susan. You did ask me to come early."

"Yes, yes! Come in!" said Susan. "Let me take your coat. The convention will not begin for hours. That leaves us ample time to exchange battle stories. Before now, our few times together have been a mad crush of activity, with precious little time for conversation."

Susan led Harriet to the parlor and poured them both some tea. "Sit, please."

"I thank you," said Harriet.

"Now, then," said Susan, settling in her chair. "Where shall we begin?"

Beginnings

Susan sipped her tea and leaned back in her rocker, flipping through memories like pages in a book.

"I started out as a teacher, did you know? I taught for fifteen years, though I could not abide the unequal pay and treatment of women in that profession. A woman might earn two-fifty a week, while a man received as much as ten dollars! The injustice of it bothered me fiercely.

"Before I retired permanently, I returned home to learn that my father, mother, and sister had attended the first Woman's Rights Convention, held in Rochester, and had signed a declaration demanding equal rights for women. It was all the talk in 1848, that and the new law allowing a woman to own real estate in her name. Mind you, until then, her husband could sell it and pocket all the money! The very idea!" Susan spat out the words. "Thinking women began to wonder what other established laws—"

"Might need fixing," suggested Harriet.

"Precisely!" said Susan. She took a deep breath. "I thought perhaps this was work I could attend to. So, in 1849, I walked away from teaching forever."

"You got the call," said Harriet, "just like Isaiah: '"Cry aloud, spare not!" says the Lord. "Lift up thy voice—"'"

"'"Like a trumpet!"'" Susan finished. She smiled and took a sip of tea.

This, thought Susan, *is going to be a most interesting afternoon.*

10

The Call

"I know about being called," said Harriet. "My call came different—first to free myself in 1849, then, once I was settled in Philadelphia, the Lord told me to free my people.

"I sorely missed the kin I'd left behind—and John, my husband. He loved the South, and being freeborn, did not feel pressed to leave it. My niece Kessiah was another matter. In 1850, I got word she was to be sold to the Deep South and would forever be lost to me, just like her own mother had been when we were children. I could not bear the thought!

"It was then the Lord whispered to me, 'Go to her,' and his voice drowned out any fear that mighta lodged itself in my heart.

"I met Kessiah and her family in Baltimore and hid them till I could get them safely 'cross the state lines. Once Kessiah was free, I set my mind on others who needed rescue."

"It would seem your destiny was clear," said Susan.

"Yes, indeed," said Harriet.

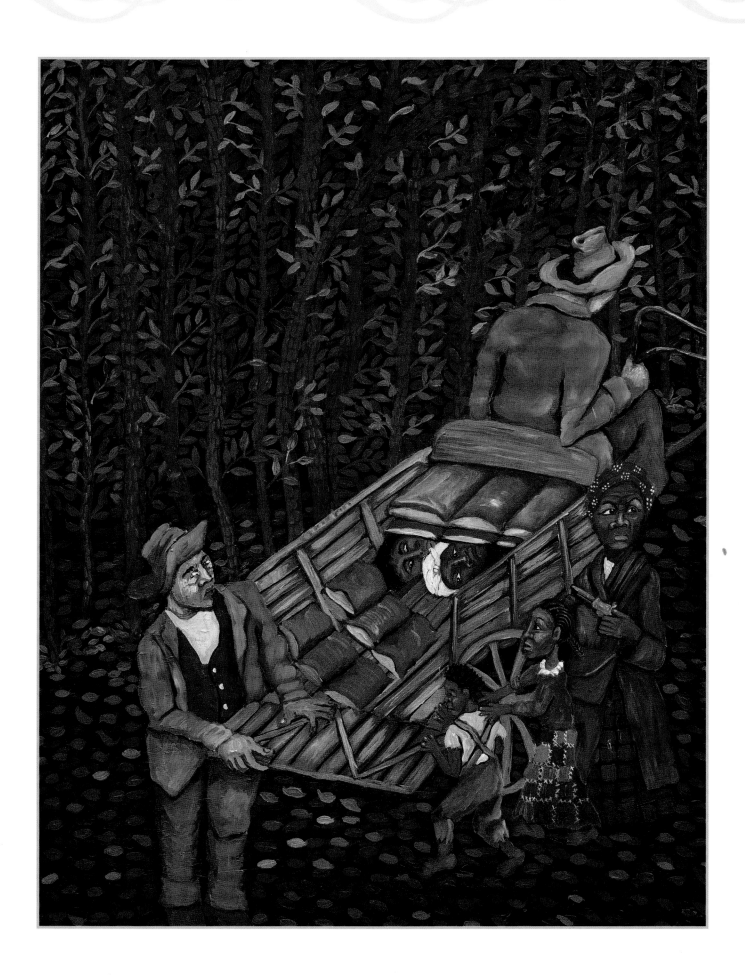

Frederick Comes to Dinner

"Freedom was much on the mind of my family," said Susan.

"There was often antislavery talk around the Anthony homestead dinner table, particularly on those Sundays when the likes of William Lloyd Garrison, Wendell Phillips, and Frederick Douglass would gather at our home, holding forth with Father for hours. But it was the evils of alcohol that most drew my attention then.

"Our towns seemed plagued by men overly fond of strong drink and whose poor wives had no legal rights to divorce them or to leave with their children, even if the women were beaten daily.

"My father, bless him, had no patience with men who drank too much and would not hire them for his factories, nor sell spirits in his store. It was a great example to me, of course. Being female myself, I felt great sympathy for the wives of these men, and determined that I must do something about their predicament.

"I joined the Daughters of Temperance, if not to end all imbibing of strong drink, then at least to win protections for the women and children it harmed."

"Lord knows, it's our hearts that drive us!" said Harriet.

The Underground Railroad

Harriet closed her eyes for a moment. When she opened them again, her focus seemed as locked in the past as the story she was telling, but then she blinked a few times and she was back.

"In spring of 1851, heartsick for my kin and grieving for their sad estate, I returned to Maryland again, this time leaving with one brother and two of his companions.

"I went south again, thinking to bring my husband John north. The risk was nearly without reward, as John had taken him a new wife and had no need of me.

"Groaning in my spirit, I sought contact with the Underground Railroad to wring some good from this journey. They helped me collect a party of eleven, and I led the way northward.

"In Rochester, I hid them at the home of Frederick Douglass till arrangements could be made for the move to Canada and freedom. By this time, I was fully committed to serve as a conductor for the Underground Railroad."

Said Susan, "As with Moses, the Creator chose your path."

Harriet nodded. "I followed it the best I could."

Speech! Speech!

"My father had prepared me to forge a path of my own choosing, having trained both daughters and sons as equals," said Susan. "Indeed, our family included 'high seat' Quakers, among them Aunt Hannah, a famous preacher, and second cousin Betsey Dunnell White, revered for her broad knowledge of politics. Many was the man in the territory who sought her out for advice. Quite naturally, then, Father encouraged me to speak my mind concerning reforms demanding attention.

"With such strong support, I overcame my early fear of speaking and publicly addressed the subject of temperance:

"'You with us, no doubt, would be most happy to speed on the time when no wife shall watch with trembling heart and tearful eye the slow, but sure descent of her . . . companion down to the loathsome haunts of drunkenness.'

"So went that first speech. It was on March 1, 1849—how could I forget? The next day, to my great surprise, many exclaimed: 'Miss Anthony is the smartest woman who ever has been in Canajoharie!'

"Once my mouth was open, I did not shut it again! I continued to speak, driven by one thought: What service can I render humanity; what can I do—"

"To change things," said Harriet.

"Yes," said Susan, "and to make them better."

"Looks like the Lord made us both servants," said Harriet. "We just had different assignments."

18

"My assignments changed from one day to the next," said Harriet. "By 1851, I set my own rhythm, traveling from Philadelphia to Maryland fall, winter, and early spring on rescue missions, then picking up work cooking and cleaning houses in Cape May through the summer, saving up and planning for the rescues to come.

"The Lord was always at my side. Once, when I was traveling by boat with a fugitive, the ticket collector told us to step aside while he took others' tickets. Tilly, the young girl with me, was all set to panic, but I gripped her hand to hold her steady, and I prayed.

"'You have been with me in six troubles,' I told the Lord. 'Do not desert me in the seventh.'

"The ticket collector let us go on, and we reached our final destination without a breath more of trouble."

"I had begun to hear of you by then," said Susan, "and to hear of the special angel who guarded you, as Thomas Garrett spoke of it. The angel who hid you from the slave catchers time and time again."

Harriet shivered, though not from the thought of slave catchers. There was a draft in the room, but Susan seemed not to notice.

The Right to Speak

"I, myself, had begun to attend antislavery conventions," said Susan, "and found my heart stirred by the words of Garrison and George Thompson. Yet my energies were committed increasingly to the rights of women.

"I joined the Teachers' Convention to speak on behalf of women workers who continued to be unfairly paid—and the injustice did not end there.

"While at the Teachers' Convention, where two-thirds of the members were women, none before me ever spoke in that assembly. When I stood and uttered my first words, 'Mr. President,' it was as if a bomb had been set off! Heads spun and chatter erupted throughout the hall.

"I had paid my fee to attend and assumed my right to speak. Yet my doing so led to thirty minutes of debate.

"At length, I was permitted to have my say. The topic was of questionable consequence, but I attended that convention every year thereafter for ten years until the ring of a woman's voice in that company became commonplace."

"I've heard you speak many a time," said Harriet. "And that voice of yours is sharp enough to slice bread and smooth enough to butter it."

"I take your compliment," said Susan.

Storyteller

"I am no speech maker, never was," said Harriet, "but I can tell a story true. Once people got wind of it, they'd pester me for details of a rescue.

"I'd pull out a story from 1852, 1853, or maybe 1854, depending on how the spirit moved me. I kept no calendar of my rescues, but I could recall every one.

"I might tell of a night spent knee-deep in a swamp, shivering in the dark till it was safe to move my party to the next station on the Underground Railroad, or of threatening to press my pistol to the temple of a runaway tempted to turn back, and whispering in his ear, 'Move or die.'

"Such stories pried open the pocketbooks of wealthy abolitionists, so I told them often to raise money for my secret journeys to and from the South."

"Your stories are the best," said Susan. "I hope to hear a few tonight! Elizabeth Cady Stanton loved them, too. We were of the same mind regarding many things, and I—I'm sorry, Harriet, but do you feel a chill?"

Harriet nodded.

"I believe I'll start a fire," said Susan.

She laid a new log in the fireplace and lit a match.

"There!" she said.

Raising a Ruckus

"Now, where was I?" asked Susan. "Oh, yes! Mrs. Stanton and I partnered together drafting speeches, sharing the lecture podium, and soliciting petition signatures.

"Thanks, in part, to our joint efforts, 28,000 petitions were presented to the Albany legislature on January 1, 1853. Along with the petitions came an appeal, elegantly penned by Mrs. Stanton, asking that women be given the vote on temperance, or else that the state should enforce Prohibition. Maine already had a law prohibiting alcohol. The response of the lawmakers made my future endeavors clear:

"'Who are these asking for a Maine law?' said a member of the legislature. 'Nobody but women and children!'

"I made a solemn vow that day that my life's work would be to make a woman's name on a petition worth as much as a man's.

"The following spring, I toured New York State alongside Amelia Bloomer and the Reverend Antoinette Brown, raising our voices on temperance and the rights of women. We were viewed as a curiosity—women who dared speak in public!"

"You were bold," said Harriet.

"Not to my thinking," said Susan. "The good Lord gave me a mouth. Was I not to use it?"

Both women chuckled. Susan got up to warm their tea.

Close Call

"I made thirteen trips south between 1850 and 1860, four in 1856 alone," said Harriet.

"You seemed a whirlwind then," said Susan. "I remember jotting in my diary how you deftly helped me fit a runaway slave for his flight to Canada."

Harriet nodded, recalling the occasion. "The stations and safe houses I used were many, but the details of each journey are with me still—most particularly, the close calls!

"Before one trip to Maryland to rescue a young woman, I got hold of a forged certificate in Philadelphia stating that I was a freeborn woman. That way I could travel by sea or rail. The Lord led me to a boat captain who provided a certificate for my runaway companion.

"We stayed the night in Seaford, Delaware, to arrange our voyage. Everything was just fine until a slave dealer at the hotel spotted us and came running in our direction.

"The hotel manager blocked the dealer's passage, and the young woman and I fled to the railroad station. I bought us two tickets to Camden and there met another conductor who carried us farther north, by wagon. Mile by mile, I saw my passenger safely to Canada."

"You were most truly a woman of adventure," said Susan.

"No," said Harriet. "More like a woman of purpose."

"I, too, found purpose," said Susan, "though I was slow to pursue the one that would most mark my life's journey—the women's vote."

Frozen Footsteps

"Among Quakers," said Susan, "not even men went to the ballot box. We thought it wrong to support a government that believed in war. Yet it became clear to me that every woman's individual right hinged on this one, single power.

"I soon found myself campaigning throughout the state, lecturing in city halls and going door-to-door with petitions demanding women's suffrage. The work was hard and often thankless.

"In the bitter winter of 1854 to 1855, the mercury fell to twelve degrees below zero. I often trudged through snowdrifts fifteen feet in height.

"I spent many a night shivering in hotel rooms without a fire and woke to find water pitchers skimmed with ice. I'd have to take my sponge and force it through to find water enough to give myself a bath! And, for all that, many a woman, seeing the petition, would slam the door in my face, saying, 'I have all the rights I need.' Yet she had not the rights to the very door she shut on me!

"I'd shake my head and move on, canvassing fifty-four counties that year alone."

The winds of autumn gathered outside. Harriet was grateful to be indoors.

A Man
Named John

"'Rest' is never a word you understood," said Harriet, "though I am no better.

"I made a home for my family in Canada, safe under the paw of the British Lion, but I tramped back and forth from the South to Ontario year after year, guiding family members and others from slavery to freedom. And did I rest there? No. I chopped wood during the long winters to earn money for food and helped recently arrived former slaves adjust to their new surroundings. Their bones were strangers to the bitter cold, and many died of pneumonia. But they all died free."

Susan nodded in silence.

"It was in Canada that John Brown came to meet me in April 1858," said Harriet. "Here was a man passionate about freedom. He said he would not even go to church with those who owned slaves. 'My knees will not bend in prayer with them while their hands are stained with the blood of souls.'

"In our first conversation, he said, 'Slavery is war.' And I agreed.

"Thereafter, he shared his plan to raid Harpers Ferry. I shared my knowledge of secret networks and transportation lines through Maryland and the Chesapeake. We pored over his plan like soldiers discussing military strategy, and he called me 'General.'

"John paid me twenty-five dollars in gold to find recruits for him in Canada among the newly freed and, of my own accord, I lectured to solicit additional funds for his operation. I had no hunger for blood, Lord knows, and I'd never been party to an uprising, but I began to understand that only strong action would bring an end to slavery.

"On the day of the raid, I lay ill in New Bedford, at the home of a friend, unaware that the attack was taking place. A stirring in my soul told me something was wrong. Then came the premonition that Captain John Brown was in trouble." Harriet hung her head. "I told my hostess that we should soon hear bad news from him. And we did."

Susan sighed. "Our John, beaten and bloody, dragged off to jail. Even now I shudder."

"My young brother Merritt nearly took part in that tragic story," said Susan. "In the spring of 1856, John Brown and his recruits spent a night in Merritt's Kansas cabin, and crept out in the early morning to raid a compound of proslavery settlers at Osawatomie Creek. Merritt was taken ill, so Mr. Brown told him to remain behind. Of course, when the sound of shots woke him, my brother ran to join in.

"Our family went weeks without knowing if Merritt was among the thirty who died or the twenty who survived!" Susan paused for a sip of tea. "The massacre Merritt saw that day soured him on violence, else he might have gone on to Harpers Ferry and joined poor John in the hangman's noose.

"On the day of John Brown's execution, with a broken heart, I held a public meeting of mourning and indignation. Scarcely three hundred attended, so afraid were most to be associated with John Brown in any way.

"I felt most alone that day.

"I sold tickets to cover the cost of the hall. I reserved for Mr. Brown's family the excess money collected."

"A kindness they long remembered," said Harriet.

"Yes? That is some comfort," said Susan.

Bounty

"I thought of John often," said Harriet, "but I kept moving forward.

"The following June, I traveled to Boston, guest of the New England Anti-Slavery Society Convention and—"

"And spoke at our special session on women's suffrage," said Susan. "I remember. The *Liberator* reported that 'Moses' spoke."

"I could not appear under my own name," said Harriet.

"Slave catchers had become more vigilant after Harpers Ferry. They waited around every corner, ready to snatch up fugitives like myself, or kidnap freeborn souls and send them into slavery as well. The Fugitive Slave Act gave them ammunition to undo the hard work of the Underground Railroad.

"I, for one, welcomed war to settle the matter of slavery. But as North and South polished their rifle muzzles, it grew harder to slip in and out of the South.

"I made one last rescue in December 1860, bringing out a couple, their two children, and another pair besides. As usual, I guided them to Canada.

"With a growing bounty on my head, my friends and family begged me to suspend my activities and remain. I finally agreed and settled for a time among the relatives I had led to freedom: my parents, my brothers James, John, and William Henry, their wives and children, and of course, Kessiah and her family."

"Ah, yes," said Susan. "Family."

Unfettered

"I chose a life without children of my own, which some considered criminal," said Susan. "Many was the insult hurled at me for remaining unmarried yet daring to speak for those with husbands.

"At one meeting, a Reverend Mayo shouted, 'You are not married. You have no business discussing marriage!' To wit, I said, 'Well, Mr. Mayo, you are not a slave. Suppose you quit lecturing on slavery!'

"I so tire of men pressing marriage. The institution has robbed our movement of many a good soldier. When I was young, one friend wed a man of feeble intellect. ''Tis strange, 'tis passing strange,' said I, 'that a girl possessed of common sense should be willing to marry a lunatic—but so it is.'

"Understand, I have nothing against marriage, but unfettered, I was free, over the years, to assemble such rousing speakers as Wendell Phillips, Lucretia Mott, and Ralph Waldo Emerson, free as well to plan conventions and gather petitions to sway our legislatures toward right action on behalf of all.

"In 1860, ten years of such effort won us passage of a law allowing a married woman full rights to dispense, manage, or collect earnings from her own property, as well as her right to joint guardianship of her children!"

"Ah, yes," said Harriet, lifting her teacup. "The law that needed fixing!"

"Precisely," said Susan.

Drums of War

"Had I remained in chains, would I have birthed children of my own with my former husband, John?" Harriet wondered. "It is a question that has often twisted my insides, though I suffer no regret of slipping from slavery's bond!

"I made a different family for myself. Having rescued my young niece Margaret, I took and raised her for my own.

"We lived peaceably in Ontario for a time. From late 1860 to spring of 1861, my rifle was left hanging on the wall unused. But I was restless, ever listening for the drums of war. The fight over slavery was a match and, soon or late, North or South would strike it."

"I, too, listened," said Susan, "though for the sound of boots approaching on the cobblestone streets, so treacherous was the mood in the cities."

She rose and went to the fireplace to warm her hands nearer the flame.

Confrontation

"I was daily vilified in the press," said Susan, "called 'brawling,' 'scum,' 'parasite,' and 'ungodly.' What was worse, filthy descriptions or the mobs?

"In 1861, when the South threatened secession and President Lincoln's reserve angered the North, we marshaled forces to call for immediate and unconditional emancipation of the slaves.

"I led a tour of lectures through New York State that year, though few of us could be heard among the mobs that met us at every city.

"In a Buffalo meeting, I stepped forward to the sounds of hiss, hoot, stomp, and yell. For two days, bedlam reigned and there was nothing for it. The police did nothing to stop the mobs. In fact, they themselves joined in, the lot of them finally rushing the platform, pressing in close with clenched fists and wild eyes.

"But I held my ground until I myself decided to declare the meeting adjourned."

Call to Arms

"At long last," said Harriet, "President Lincoln gave the call to arms, and Governor John Andrew of Massachusetts summoned me to help support the Union by joining his contingent on the move south.

"We slowly made our way to Beaufort, South Carolina, where I served in the Union Army Camp as nurse, cook, and spy. There, Colonel Robert Gould Shaw and his all-black Massachusetts Fifty-fourth Regiment gathered and prepared for an attack on Fort Wagner, hoping to prove themselves by wresting victory for the Union.

"At first light, the day of the operation, I served the colonel a hot breakfast."

"Not knowing it would be his last," added Susan.

"That evening," continued Harriet, "after witnessing the carnage that whittled the Fifty-fourth from 650 to 378, I held back my tears and attended to the survivors. One of them went by the name of Private Lewis Douglass—"

"Frederick's son!" said Susan.

"The same," said Harriet. "I bandaged his wounds, and he spoke most proudly of those who fell around him that day. 'Not a man flinched,' he said. Others said the same of him.

"Lord! Frederick had him a son he could boast of," said Harriet. Susan smiled.

World Afire

"Freedom was close," said Susan, "but not yet won. My help was increasingly sought in forwarding the fight toward full emancipation of The Slave. I lectured with Horace Greeley, Garrison, and Douglass.

"The fight for women's rights was set aside, though only briefly. Unlike others of my sex, I was not convinced that the freedom of the slaves would immediately lead to women's suffrage. Nonetheless, I joined Mrs. Stanton to form the National Loyal League of Women, calling others to stand with us.

"I daily dispatched workers to fill petitions we'd present to Lincoln, proving our support. We attended to this necessary work in the midst of the New York draft riots when rocks, as well as ugly words, were hurled.

"These were terrible times, during which the Colored Orphan Asylum was burned to the ground, barely one city block from Mrs. Stanton's home!

"Some days, we were unable to reach our offices in safety.

"I trembled in fear for our nation."

46

End of the Beginning

"And here we are in 1904," said Harriet, "survivors of the war. There remains much to do, helping the needy, the disabled veterans, the orphans, and the homeless. Some need more help than others, so I continue to struggle on their behalf. Who will care for them if we do not?

"As for the rights of women—a reporter asked me whether I believed females should have the vote. I raised my head up, high as I could, and answered, 'I suffered enough to believe it.'"

"Indeed!" said Susan.

"So I continue speaking, and will speak for the rights of my people, and the rights of women, as long as God gives me breath."

"And we are glad for it!" said Susan. "Oh, dear! Our reminiscences have carried us late into the day. Come! Your audience is waiting. We have yet more work to do, you and I.

"Emancipation is secure, but not the vote! Until we have it," said Susan, "we're not done chasing freedom."

"Then let's get to it!" said Harriet.

Biographies

- John Albion Andrew (1818–1867) was governor of Massachusetts from 1861 to 1866. Strongly in favor of the emancipation of the slave, he was aware of Harriet Tubman and her work on the Underground Railroad. As soon as President Lincoln gave the call to arms that began the Civil War, Andrew organized the Massachusetts militia and they were the first to join the Union Army.

- Susan Brownell Anthony (1820–1906), a prominent figure in the antislavery movement, was best known as a pioneer and leader in the struggle for women's rights in the United States. Together with Elizabeth Cady Stanton, Anthony founded the first women's temperance movement; started the women's rights journal the *Revolution*; and wrote a draft of an amendment to give  women the vote. Constantly traveling from city to city with her messages, Anthony gave an average of seventy-five to one hundred speeches per year. Though she did not live to see the women's vote (the Nineteenth Amendment) enacted, no one worked harder to secure it.

- Antoinette Brown Blackwell (1825–1921) was the United States' first female ordained pastor. In addition to preaching sermons in Congregational and, later, Unitarian pulpits around the country, she was a frequent speaker on the antislavery and women's rights circuits.

- Amelia Jenks Bloomer (1818–1894) believed women's clothing should be as practical and comfortable as men's attire. She came up with a design of her own, which came to be known as "bloomers." The design proved very controversial at the time and never caught on. Bloomer was part of Susan B. Anthony's inner circle.

- John Brown (1800–1859) was a militant abolitionist, best known as the architect and leader of the failed Harpers Ferry raid of 1859. Brown believed that strong actions would motivate slaves to rise up against their owners and bring an end to slavery. His passion for the freedom of black people and his bold actions on their behalf led Tubman to say of him, "When I think how he gave up his life for our people, and how he never flinched, but was so brave to the end; it's clear to me it wasn't mortal man, it was God in him."

- Frederick Douglass (1819?–1895) was born into slavery, but escaped in 1838. He went on to carve a place for himself in American history as an orator; publisher of the weekly antislavery newspaper the *North Star*; and author of three biographies, the best known titled *Narrative of the Life of Frederick Douglass, An American Slave, Written by Himself*. An eloquent speaker against slavery and for women's rights, Douglass advocated for the inclusion of freed black men in the Union Army. Douglass helped form the Massachusetts Fifty-fourth Regiment, in which two of his sons, Lewis and Charles, served bravely. Douglass was a close friend of the Anthony family and a colleague of Harriet Tubman.

- Ralph Waldo Emerson (1803–1882) was an essayist, poet, anthologist, and lecturer. A leading voice in American culture, he favored individualism and freedom. He gave his first rousing antislavery speech in 1838, in reaction to the brutal mob murder of abolitionist and publisher Elijah P. Lovejoy. He later became an ardent abolitionist himself.

- Thomas Garrett (1789–1871) was a Quaker merchant and Delaware stationmaster for the Underground Railroad. Garrett opened his home to runaway slaves almost daily, hiding them briefly until they could continue to the next safe house on their journey. Arrested for the crime of harboring fugitives, Garrett was given fines high enough to leave him bankrupt. Still, he continued his work for the Underground Railroad, alongside Harriet Tubman.

- William Lloyd Garrison (1805–1879), publisher of the *Liberator*, a weekly antislavery newspaper, was a staunch abolitionist. In 1832, he founded the New England Anti-Slavery Society and was a frequent speaker at its conventions.

- Horace Greeley (1811–1872) was the founder and editor of the *New York Tribune*, which he launched in 1841. Greeley turned the *Tribune* into one of the most politically important newspapers of the North, using its pages to promote his strong antislavery stance. He also supported the rights of women and wrote favorably of Susan B. Anthony and other active feminists, often joining them on the platform at their conventions.

- Lucretia Mott (1793–1880) was an outspoken Quaker minister who joined Elizabeth Cady Stanton in calling for the Seneca Falls Convention in New York, the first women's rights convention. The declarations made at Seneca Falls launched the women's suffrage movement. Mott was a popular speaker during the early days of the movement, calling both for women's rights and an end to slavery. Mott was a friend and colleague of Susan B. Anthony.

- Wendell Phillips (1811–1884) was an American abolitionist, with a reputation as a keen, brilliant, and passionate orator. Phillips was a frequent speaker at antislavery conventions and became president of the American Anti-Slavery Society in 1865. He was a fervent supporter of temperance and women's rights. Further, he was outspoken on the importance of women's suffrage.

- Robert Gould Shaw (1837–1863) was the commander of the Massachusetts Fifty-fourth Regiment, an all-black regiment formed during the Civil War just after the signing of the Emancipation Proclamation. Shaw, only twenty-five years old, died with many of his men when they stormed Fort Wagner, South Carolina. The film *Glory* is based on his story.

- Elizabeth Cady Stanton (1815–1902) was one of the chief architects of the Declaration of Sentiments. This writer, editor, and activist was a close friend and collaborator of Susan B. Anthony. The two women frequently shared the stage as they toured the country, speaking for women's rights and against slavery.

- George D. Thompson (1804–1878) was an English-born abolitionist and a member of the British Parliament. He made his mark as an antislavery activist and speaker, both in England and the United States.

- Harriet Tubman (1820?–1913) was born Araminta Ross, a slave. When she escaped to freedom in 1849, she took on her mother's first name, Harriet, and kept the surname of her first husband, John Tubman. A famed conductor on the Underground Railroad, Tubman was a prominent voice in the antislavery movement and the women's rights movement as well. During the Civil War, she worked as cook, nurse, army scout, and spy for Union forces. Later in life, she continued to speak on behalf of women's rights, raised funds to help support former slaves, and founded a home for elderly African Americans in Auburn, New York. The one thing Tubman never did was stand still. Long dubbed "Moses" and "General," Harriet Tubman received many honors during her life and after her death. In March 1913 she was buried with military honors at Fort Hill Cemetery in Auburn, New York.

Additional Notes

- The Declaration of Sentiments of 1848, signed by sixty-eight women and thirty-two men, was the basis for seeking civil, social, political, and religious rights of women. This launched the women's rights movement. The primary author of the declaration was Elizabeth Cady Stanton, who based its form on the Declaration of Independence.

- The Dred Scott Decision, 1857, was the Supreme Court ruling that said people of African descent, whether enslaved or free, were not protected by the Constitution and could never be U.S. citizens. Further, it justified the enslavement of people of African descent. When the Fourteenth Amendment was passed in 1868, stating that all persons born or naturalized in the United States are citizens of the United States, the Dred Scott Decision was effectively overruled.

- The Emancipation Proclamation, signed by President Lincoln in 1863, declared the full and unconditional freedom of slaves in the Confederate States.

- The Fugitive Slave Act of 1850 stated that all runaway slaves must be brought back to their owners, whether they were found in the North or South. Slaves and abolitionists called it the Bloodhound Law because slave catchers often used dogs to track down runaways. Law enforcement officers who did not arrest suspected runaways could be fined $1,000, while officers who did capture and return slaves could receive a bonus or promotion for doing so. This legislation made the work of the Underground Railroad more difficult than ever, and thousands of newly freed blacks migrated to Canada to escape the law's reach.

- The Harpers Ferry Raid of 1859 was an attack on the federal arsenal at Harpers Ferry by militant abolitionist John Brown and a handful of his followers. Originally, Brown had planned to stage guerrilla warfare in the hills of the Blue Ridge Mountains, using them as a stage to incite a slave insurrection. He believed launching attacks on slaveholders would stir the slaves to action. However, one of his followers betrayed him by revealing the plan, and Brown was forced to go into hiding. One year later, he devised a second, more desperate plan to raid Harpers Ferry. Many friends warned him against it, but he would not be dissuaded. Ten out of twenty-two men died in the failed attempt, including two of Brown's own sons. Brown was quickly tried, sentenced, and executed for his crime.

- The Kansas-Nebraska Act, 1854, gave each new state or territory the right to choose whether or not to allow slavery within its borders. Antislavery and proslavery settlers along the Kansas-Nebraska border fought violently over this, leading to what was alternately called Bloody Kansas, Bleeding Kansas, the Kansas-Nebraska War, or the Border War.

- The *Liberator* (1831–1865) was an abolitionist newspaper founded by William Lloyd Garrison, considered the leader of one of the most radical divisions of white abolitionists. The *Liberator* came to be known for its uncompromising call for immediate emancipation of all slaves.

- The Maine Law of 1851 was a law that prohibited sales of alcohol, unless they were for medicinal or other useful purposes. By 1855, twelve states had joined Maine in total prohibition. These were referred to as "dry" states. Riots against the law led to its being partially repealed in 1856.

- The New York draft riots of July 13–16, 1863, erupted when laborers protested against a new law passed by Congress to draft men for the Civil War. Poor and working-class men, who generally earned less than $500 a year, resented the fact that wealthier men were allowed to pay a fee of $300 to avoid the draft altogether. Men took to the streets to show their anger. These same men feared that newly freed black men might compete for their jobs and, as a result, the protests against the draft expanded into an ugly race war. At the height of it, an orphanage for black children was burned to the ground. The orphanage was located one block from the home of Elizabeth Cady Stanton. President Lincoln had to send militia and volunteer troops to control the city.

- Quakers are members of the Religious Society of Friends, a Christian denomination. They are known for pacifism, simplicity of lifestyle, integrity, and a belief in social and racial equality. Many extended help to fugitive slaves, offering their homes as stations on the Underground Railroad. Susan B. Anthony's strong Quaker upbringing gave her an inclination for issues of social justice. Harriet Tubman relied on many Quakers for help in her work of rescuing slaves from the South.

- Secession Declarations (1860–1861) were documents filed individually by several southern states, including Mississippi, South Carolina, Texas, and Georgia. The documents explain each state's reasons for seceding, or separating, from the United States. Between 1860 and 1861, eleven states seceded and formed the Confederate States of America. These proslavery states did not wish to be governed by an antislavery president (Lincoln) and his administration. It took the Civil War to both abolish slavery and unify the nation.

- The temperance movement was an effort driven by the church to moderate or eliminate the consumption of alcohol. Leaders of the movement pushed the government to create anti-alcohol legislation. Susan B. Anthony quickly realized that women were not allowed a voice in the existing temperance societies and, in response, formed the Daughters of Temperance.

- Women's suffrage is the right of women to vote and to run for office. The Nineteenth Amendment, ratified in 1920, secured this right. Though Susan B. Anthony devoted her life to the hard work of attaining the vote for women in the United States, neither she nor fellow worker Harriet Tubman lived long enough to see it enacted. Yet the pioneering work of these women paved the way for congresswomen and female senators, Supreme Court justices, and secretaries-of-state to follow.

Bibliography

- Clinton, Catherine. *Harriet Tubman: The Road to Freedom*. New York: Back Bay, 2005.
- Gordon, Ann D., ed. *The Selected Papers of Elizabeth Cady Stanton and Susan B. Anthony*. Vol. 1, *In the School of Anti-Slavery, 1840–1866*. New Brunswick: Rutgers University, 1997.
- Hagedorn, Ann. *Beyond the River: The Untold Story of the Heroes of the Underground Railroad*. New York: Simon & Schuster, 2002.
- Harper, Ida Husted. *The Life and Work of Susan B. Anthony*. Vol. 1. 1899.
- Humez, Jean M. *Harriet Tubman: The Life and the Life Stories*. Madison: University of Wisconsin Press, 2004.
- Parker, John P. *His Promised Land: The Autobiography of John P. Parker, Former Slave and Conductor on the Underground Railroad*. Edited by Stuart Seely Sprague. New York: W. W. Norton, 1996.
- Still, William. *The Underground Railroad: Authentic Narratives and First-hand Accounts*. Edited by Ian Finseth. 1872. Reprint, Mineola, NY: Dover, 2007.
- Sunderland, La Roy. *Anti Slavery Manual: Containing a Collection of Facts and Arguments on American Slavery*. 1837.
- Tobin, Jacqueline L. *From Midnight to Dawn: The Last Tracks of the Underground Railroad*. New York: Anchor, 2007.
- Ward, Geoffrey C., and Ken Burns. *Not for Ourselves Alone: The Story of Elizabeth Cady Stanton and Susan B. Anthony*. New York: Knopf, 1999.

Author's Note

In 1988, I was asked to write a series of dramatic monologues for a theater group headed to China. The monologues were to be incorporated into a play about American heroes. I chose Harriet Tubman, Susan B. Anthony, and Frederick Douglass as my subjects.

In the process of researching these individuals, I was astounded to learn that they all knew one another, and that they were part of a larger circle of historical luminaries with whom I was familiar. This was a wonderful surprise to me, because history is often taught in isolated bits and pieces, and students rarely get the notion that these bits and pieces are connected. In fact, most of the time, we don't realize which historical figures were alive at the same time, nor do we get the picture of them working together and influencing one another.

These new insights made me tingle. I began to wonder what it would be like to get some of these characters in the same room. I wondered, for instance, if Tubman and Anthony had ever had a conversation and, if so, what it might have sounded like. I couldn't get the idea out of my head.

I finished writing my monologues, went to China as part of the theater troupe myself, and went on to many more adventures. Meanwhile, my idea lay sleeping in memory, waiting for attention. More than twenty years would pass before I'd take that idea out and brush it off. *Chasing Freedom* is the result.

Chasing Freedom is a work of historical fiction. The conversation between Tubman and Anthony is an imaginary one. There are historically documented encounters between the two women, most of which took place at antislavery and women's rights conventions where both women were in attendance, either as guests or speakers. During at least two of these meetings, Anthony introduced Tubman to the audience. However, there is no historical evidence of a lengthy conversation between them, nor did I come across evidence of any social encounter in Anthony's or Tubman's homes.

All of the content of this imaginary conversation is based on historical fact—stories of the Underground Railroad, the relationships between Tubman, Anthony, and all of the prominent figures mentioned, the appearance of mobs at some of Anthony's meetings, the Kansas-Nebraska border war, the draft riots of New York City.

The women's suffrage convention of 1904, in Rochester, New York, actually took place. However, I could find no indication of the precise month in which it occurred. For the purposes of my story, I chose November.

Anthony was a scheduled speaker at this event, while Tubman had originally planned only to attend. However, an impromptu introduction by Anthony led to Tubman's speaking at length. It was on this occasion, speaking of her tenure as a conductor on the Underground Railroad, that Tubman famously said, "I never ran my train off the track and I never lost a passenger."

The Rochester home at which the imaginary conversation took place was the actual residence of Anthony. Photographs of her parlor can be found online. My descriptions of the meeting site were drawn from those photos.

I've captured the voice of each woman as best I can, drawing on historical quotes and, in the case of Anthony, diary excerpts.

At the point that my story ends, the women's vote had not yet been attained. I decided to end the story at that point because neither woman lived to see this right made into law. Yet both women worked toward it until the last breath, never ceasing to chase this one, final freedom.

I hope you've enjoyed *Chasing Freedom*. I created this conversation as a way to bring the stories of Tubman and Anthony to life, and to show the ways in which their lives, and the lives of other prominent figures of the late 1800s and early 1900s, were interwoven. Connections between the great abolitionists of the day, the great authors of the day, the great suffragettes of the day, and the great politicians of the day are connections that make me, as a reader, excited about history. After reading this book, perhaps you'll be excited about history, too.

There is so much more to learn about Harriet Tubman and Susan B. Anthony. Peel back the pages of history and see what you can find on your own!